For Mary Ulm Mayhew, a spirit
filled with paint-box colors
—B.J.

For the huggable Glen
and the squeezable Pat
—R.A.

 little bee books

An imprint of Bonnier Publishing USA
251 Park Avenue South, New York, NY 10010
Text copyright © 2017 by Barbara Joosse
Illustrations copyright © 2017 by Rebecca Ashdown
All rights reserved, including the right of reproduction in whole or in part in
any form. LITTLE BEE BOOKS is a trademark of Bonnier Publishing USA, and
associated colophon is a trademark of Bonnier Publishing USA.
Manufactured in China   LEO 1116
First Edition 10 9 8 7 6 5 4 3 2 1
ISBN 978-1-4998-0404-1
Library of Congress Cataloging-in-Publication Data
Names: Joosse, Barbara M., author. | Ashdown, Rebecca, illustrator.
Title: Wally wants to hug / by Barbara Joosse; illustrated by Rebecca Ashdown.
Description: First Edition. | New York : Little Bee Books, [2017]
Summary: Wally is a young boa constrictor who loves hugs, but his classmates at school are scared
of getting hugs from him, so Wally shows them his friendly hugs are nothing to be afraid of.
Identifiers: LCCN 2016014965 Subjects: | CYAC: Boa constrictor–Fiction. | Snakes–Fiction.
Hugging–Fiction. | Schools–Fiction. Classification: LCC PZ7.J7435 Wal 2017 | DDC [E]–dc23
LC record available at https://lccn.loc.gov/2016014965

littlebeebooks.com
bonnierpublishingusa.com

WALLY
WANTS TO
HUG

by Barbara Joosse

illustrated by
Rebecca Ashdown

little bee books

Wally was a boa constrictor who loved to hug.

Every morning Mom hugged the sleepies out of Wally and his brother, Bob.

"Hugging's the way to start the day!"

And at night, Dad hugged the sleepies back in.

"Sleep tight!"

But things were different away from home.
At school, when Wally tried to give Bella a "birthday hug"...

Kitty

Bella

"Bella...?"

...she hid in her cubby.

And when he tried to give Tom a "welcome back hug"...

"Hellooo?"

...Tom pulled himself in.

At Sharing Time, Henry showed his sock puppet.

Afterward, everyone gave Henry a "hooray hug."

Sssssigh.

Everyone except Wally.

That night, Wally talked to his family.
"Everyone runs away when
I try to hug them.
Why do they do that?"

"We're boa constrictors," said Bob.
"We squeeze our food. Hard!"

"Pssh," said Dad.
"Wally knows the difference
between food and friends."

"Just be your cuddly self, Wally,"
said Mom. "Soon your friends
will let you hug."

The next day at school, it was Wally's turn to share.

He made himself into
a mountain . . .

a tree . . .

and a house.

Everyone clapped.

But nobody hugged.

Then Wally made himself
into a teardrop.

"Let's let Wally know how much we like him,"
said Miss Carmen.

"I think
you're great."

Wally felt loved. But he also felt sad.
Tears slid down Wally's cheeks.

"He wants
to hug."

"Wally's crying."

"Yeah, but . . ."

"Wally, I think your friends think
you'll hug too hard," said Miss Carmen.
"Do you promise not to squeeze?"

"I promise."

Then the friends huddled together
and hugged Wally.

And Wally hugged them back.
Gently.

But then Wally got carried away.
He couldn't help himself.

So he gave everyone a big . . .